Fire on the Mountain

Pamela McDowell

illustrated by
Dana Barton

orca Echoes

ORCA BOOK PUBLISHERS

To my mom and dad,
who always believed I could. —P.M.

Text copyright © Pamela McDowell 2022
Illustrations copyright © Dana Barton 2022

Published in Canada and the United States in 2022 by Orca Book Publishers.
orcabook.com

Library and Archives Canada Cataloguing in Publication
Title: Fire on the mountain / Pamela McDowell ; illustrated by Dana Barton.
Names: McDowell, Pamela, author. | Barton, Dana, illustrator.
Series: Orca echoes.
Description: Series statement: Orca echoes
Identifiers: Canadiana (print) 20210167114 | Canadiana (ebook) 20210167122 |
ISBN 9781459826144 (softcover) | ISBN 9781459826151 (PDF) | ISBN 9781459826168 (EPUB)
Classification: LCC PS8625.D785 F57 2022 | DDC jC813/.6—dc23

Library of Congress Control Number: 2021934064

Summary: In this illustrated early chapter book, a forest fire threatens the town
of Waterton, and Cricket and her brother do their best to save their home.

Orca Book Publishers is committed to reducing the consumption of
nonrenewable resources in the making of our books. We make every
effort to use materials that support a sustainable future.

Orca Book Publishers gratefully acknowledges the support for its publishing
programs provided by the following agencies: the Government of Canada,
the Canada Council for the Arts and the Province of British Columbia
through the BC Arts Council and the Book Publishing Tax Credit.

Cover artwork and interior illustrations by Dana Barton
Author photo by Mirror Image Photography
Edited by Liz Kemp

Printed and bound in Canada.

25 24 23 22 • 1 2 3 4

Cricket McKay series

Ospreys in Danger
Salamander Rescue
Bats in Trouble
Cougar Frenzy

Chapter One

"Thunderstorms are the worst." Shilo crossed her arms and stared out the window. The clouds had been building all afternoon, and now the sky looked gray and menacing.

"Uh-huh," Cricket said. She studied the Jenga tower, not really listening. "Can you turn on the light? It's hard to see the game."

"That's because of the stupid storm," Shilo grumbled as she turned on the lamp. She watched Cricket slide a wooden block out of the stack and place it carefully on top. Thunder rumbled, bouncing between the mountains.

Cricket had lived in the little town of Waterton, in the middle of Waterton Lakes National Park, all her life. Thunderstorms in September were normal after a hot summer. She kind of liked the storms, especially at night, when she could burrow down safe and warm in her blankets and watch out her window as lightning crackled in the sky. The sound of rain pounding on the roof would lull her to sleep.

"What I don't get is why we have thunderstorms almost every day, but no rain." Cricket watched as Shilo tapped a block and eased it from the bottom as the tower swayed.

"Yeah, it's so dry, the grass is crunchy. I had to wear shoes almost all summer," Shilo said.

Cricket pinched her nose and waved her hand. "Lucky for us," she said and

laughed when Shilo rolled her eyes. Cricket focused on the Jenga tower again. She tapped a block, then gripped it carefully and wiggled it free.

Ka-boom!

A flash of lightning lit up the room at the same time as thunder cracked, shaking the house.

"Ah!" Cricket jumped, and the tower fell. Wooden blocks scattered across the floor. The lights flickered and went out.

"Not again," Shilo groaned.

Seconds later the lights came back on, though they were a little dimmer than before.

Shilo turned to Cricket. "What...?"

"It's the emergency generator." Cricket stood up, and Shilo followed her to the kitchen, where Warden McKay was working on a computer.

Cricket's dad was a park warden in Waterton Lakes National Park. It was his job to sort out disagreements between wildlife and tourists. The week before, he had helped a family that discovered a porcupine had moved into their tent and was refusing to leave. As the weather got hotter and the forest got drier, he spent more time checking campfires and reminding visitors how to extinguish them properly.

Shilo peered over Warden McKay's shoulder at the screen. "That's cool. Is it part of Waterton? And what are those little dots? They keep changing color."

Warden McKay shook his head. "Waterton is down here," he said, pointing to the corner of the screen. "These are the mountains west of us, and those dots are lightning strikes. This website tracks the direction of the storm and helps us predict where forest fires might start. With some luck, we can put them out before they get too big."

Thunder cracked and rumbled, and a fresh flurry of dots sprinkled the map. Warden McKay frowned and scribbled some notes.

"Is that bad, Dad?"

"It's certainly not good," he said. "Not good at all."

Chapter Two

The next day, school seemed to be dragging on forever. Cricket couldn't stop yawning in science class. Shilo made a face at her and wiggled her eyebrows.

"Dad left really early this morning," Cricket whispered, "in the helicopter."

In fact, he had left twice. Cricket had heard him start the truck just before dawn, when the sky outside her window was still inky black. Not long after that the helicopter had flown over their house, taking the crew out to check on the lightning strikes.

"He came back, then left again just before breakfast," she whispered, while

Mr. Tanaka drew a diagram of a cell that looked a lot like a fried egg. "That time he was going to find some hikers in the backcountry."

"Are you kidding?" Shilo whispered. "It's so dry, the trails have been closed for weeks! How did they get in there without seeing the signs? I'll bet your dad was mad about that."

Cricket shrugged. "He just wants to find them. He's worried that if a fire starts, it'll move pretty quickly and could trap them."

Shilo snorted. "So he's got to risk his life to rescue those dummies?"

A commotion near the windows drew everyone's attention. Even Mr. Tanaka abandoned his lesson to have a look. A herd of deer raced across the school field, heading toward the lake.

"Wow, there's so many!"

"Look at all the babies!"

"Is something chasing them?"

The deer headed right into town. After the herd disappeared, the kids kept watching, waiting to see what had been chasing them. Was it a bear? A wolf? A cougar?

Nothing. Eventually the excitement died down, and the kids moved back to their seats. The day continued to drag on for Cricket.

On their way home from school, the girls paused to let a couple of bighorn sheep and a lamb cross the street in front of them. The ewes stared at the girls with their weird amber eyes, then turned and dashed across Mrs. Steeves's lawn.

"Wow!" Shilo bounced up and down, spinning around, looking for more sheep. "Those guys don't come to town very often."

"It seems like all the animals are on the move," Cricket said. "Do you think they're evacuating or something?"

Shilo nodded. "Maybe, but your dad didn't say anything about a fire near here, did he? The lightning strikes were far away."

"Yeah." Cricket was frowning as she stared at Bertha Peak, feeling the hot wind on her face. What if a fire *did* come close to the town?

"I've never been evacuated before," Shilo said. "Where do you think we'd go? Pincher Creek would be okay. We could stay at the community center and go swimming every day and go to the library. That would be kinda fun, right?" Shilo nodded to herself. "I wouldn't mind that, but my mom would probably make us stay at Aunt Tina's." She made a face. "She's got a lot of rules. Where do you think you'd go?"

Cricket shrugged. "Probably my grandpa's farm," she said, but she wasn't really worried about where they'd go. If no one was left to protect their town, what would happen if the fire came close? And what would happen to all the animals?

At dinner that night, Cricket's dad confirmed that the lightning strikes had started a fire far outside the park.

"In fact, the storm started a few small fires last night. We put most of them out with the helicopter bucket, but one was already too big for that."

"But you said the fire is far away, right? It's nowhere near here, is it?"

Cricket felt worry flutter in her stomach. Suddenly she wasn't hungry anymore. She described the way the deer had been acting in the morning, and the sheep after school.

Her dad frowned. "Unfortunately wind pushed the fire up to the Continental Divide today. It's a lot closer than when it started. Most animals, even bugs, can sense the smoke before we can, and for many of them, their instinct is to run or fly away."

Cricket put down her fork. Something really had been chasing the deer, but it wasn't a predator—it was smoke.

"Fire in the forest isn't a bad thing," Warden McKay said. "In fact, fire helps the forest stay healthy. But if wind keeps pushing it, the fire could threaten the town."

Chapter Three

That night Cricket tossed and turned. She knew not all the animals could outrun the fire. Like her dad had said, deer and birds were escaping early, but what about the bigger, slower animals? She thought of big old Samson, the grizzly that lived close to town but never caused more trouble than a traffic jam. How fast could he run? And would he know where to go?

She rolled over and watched the trees outside her window. Would the porcupines know where to go? When they are afraid, porcupines climb trees just like squirrels do, hiding in the highest branches.

That would be a terrible place to hide in a fire! Cricket squeezed her eyes closed. How many animals would try to hide instead of run? What would the salamanders and snakes do? Could they go deep enough underground to stay cool?

Crying, Cricket threw off the covers. She got out of bed and stood at her window, watching the moon. There were no clouds in the sky, which meant no rain, and the trees were still. Without wind to push it, maybe the fire would stay on the far side of the mountain. Maybe it would burn itself out, even without rain. She dried her eyes and crawled back into bed, imagining the fire fizzling to a puff of smoke.

Early the next morning, the house was quiet. Cricket had just finished getting dressed when Tyler knocked and poked his head into her room.

"You ready? We've got a ton of chores to do, so let's go!"

Cricket raised her eyebrows in surprise. Where was Mom? What about school? And what about breakfast? Before she could ask, Tyler handed her a peanut butter sandwich and took off down the hall.

Outside, Cricket found her mom carrying a ladder and leaf blower from the garage. She leaned the ladder against the house and held it as Tyler climbed up and onto the roof. Then she handed him the leaf blower and earmuffs.

"What's going on?" Cricket asked. "Don't we have to go to school?"

Mrs. McKay shook her head. "Not today. If the wind gets blowing today, the fire could move again."

"But shouldn't we leave? If the fire is coming, shouldn't we go?"

"Dad will tell us when it's time to go. Don't worry—he'll be sure we're safe." Her mom gave her a hug. "For now, there's work to do."

Cricket followed her to the back of the house. "But if we're lucky, they'll put the fire out. Or maybe it will start to rain. Or maybe the wind will change direction."

Her mom nodded. "There is some luck involved with fire, but there is also a lot we can do to protect ourselves and the town."

They heard the whine of the leaf blower as Tyler started clearing leaves and pine needles off the roof.

"We can start by protecting our house." Her mom lifted a chair from the deck. "You can help me move everything into the garage."

They worked together for an hour, moving patio furniture and trimming all

the tall grass at the edges of the yard and under trees.

"What about your tree house, Cricket? Is there anything in there that we need to move?"

She shook her head. "Not much. Maybe a blanket."

Cricket climbed up the ladder that she and Shilo had nailed together the previous summer. The wood felt dry and splintery—like it would burn in a flash if the fire even looked at it. She poked her head into the tree house and took a quick look around. There was no furniture in the little hideout, just the blanket she remembered, balled up in the corner.

As she reached for it, the blanket moved. Cricket froze.

"Anything up there? Do you need some help?" her mom called.

"Um…no?" Cricket held her breath. The blanket moved again, and a dark brown nose poked out, snuffling at her. Two small brown eyes blinked. And then she saw the quills.

Cricket gave a little squeak and scrambled back down the ladder.

"It's a porcupine! It's got my blanket." She looked back over her shoulder as if she expected to see the porcupine following her down the ladder.

"Cool!" Tyler put down the rake and started taking off his work gloves.

"No. We need to leave that poor thing alone," Mrs. McKay said. "It's probably scared and trying to find a safe place to hide."

Cricket frowned. The tree house wasn't going to be a safe place if the fire got close. But there wasn't much she could do to help. His eyes looked friendly, but the quills did not.

Tyler pouted and picked up the rake.

"Let's have some lunch," Mrs. McKay said, "and plan our next move."

Chapter Four

In the middle of lunch, Mrs. McKay dashed off to help at the warden's office. All the files and office equipment there had to be packed up and ready for evacuation.

Cricket finished her sandwich and watched Tyler trying to balance a cracker on his nose. If this were a normal day, she'd be in school, having lunch with Shilo and their friends—not watching Tyler trying to balance a cracker on his nose. She sighed. Did she *really* miss school already?

Wait. Cricket sat up straight. What about the school? Would anyone trim the long grass around the playground? Would anyone make sure *it* was fire ready? She gulped down her milk and stood up. The cracker dropped from Tyler's nose.

"Come on, Tyler, let's go!" Cricket stuffed some water bottles into her backpack and headed out the door, explaining her plan as they grabbed their work gloves from the garage.

As they walked to the school, Cricket was amazed by the busyness in the town. People were working in their yards or on their roofs, and the sounds of leaf blowers and chain saws vibrated through the streets. Worry fluttered in Cricket's stomach again. The fire must be getting closer.

"I can't believe we're going back to school on a day off," Tyler grumbled.

Cricket rolled her eyes. "Not really," she said. "Besides, everyone else is super busy with other things, so it's up to us."

"I thought you'd say that," Tyler said, "so I called some friends."

Shilo and Tyler's friend Will met them at the playground, carrying rakes and gloves. They all worked for an hour, cutting the tall grass and ripping out the weeds beside the school, around the playground and along the fences. Tyler and Shilo raked everything into a pile to be picked up by one of the national park's trucks.

The kids flopped down in the shade beside the school. Cricket gulped down her entire bottle of water. Shilo nudged her with an elbow and looked over at Tyler. Cricket's brother was slowly dribbling his water onto his head, letting it roll down his face and ears, soaking his shirt. Cricket rolled her eyes.

Will watched a group of people near Cameron Falls. "Who are those guys?"

he asked. They wore dark gray pants, red shirts and yellow helmets—definitely not tourists.

"They're not all guys," Shilo said.

The kids scrambled to their feet, picked up their tools and walked down the block toward Cameron Falls. The group was unloading equipment from a truck and carrying large coils of hose up the trail. The flutter of worry moved from Cricket's stomach to just below her ribs. She recognized their uniforms—they were firefighters. As the kids approached, the team stopped for a water break.

One of the firefighters waved and smiled. "Hey, what are you all doing out here? It looks like you've been working." She took off her helmet and wiped her forehead with her arm. On her shoulder was the crest of the Lethbridge Fire Department.

"Yeah, we cleaned up the schoolyard," Cricket said. "What are you doing? Did my dad call you? He's the park warden."

The firefighter nodded. "We got the call this morning and gathered up all the hose and pumps the department could spare. We're going to lay hose all along the slope behind Evergreen Avenue, from Cameron Bay to Emerald Bay."

"That's a long way!" Tyler said. "It's got to be about a mile."

"Yup. And we'll lay smaller hose off that main line so we can soak the forest and the houses along this edge of town." She turned to Cricket. "I'm Firefighter Whitney. Are you Warden McKay's daughter?"

Cricket nodded and introduced Tyler and their friends. She stopped when two helicopters roared overhead.

"Is the fire close? Do we need to evacuate?" Shilo asked.

"It hasn't moved much," Whitney said. "It's good that the wind has died down and the air teams can work on it."

Cricket nodded. Light winds never lasted long in Waterton. Their town was in the windiest corner of Alberta, where high winds caused trees to grow crooked and waves to crash on the shore of the lake, just like at the ocean. And she knew the wind could change quickly, blasting down the valley, picking up tents that weren't tied down properly and sending unmoored boats to the end of the lake. The wind would come—but they didn't know when or which way it would blow.

"Can we help?" Tyler looked more excited and less worried than Cricket felt.

Whitney shook her head. "No, not out here." She paused. "But there is something we need. We left Lethbridge without packing a lot of food. We've got

enough for today, but we'll be looking for lunch tomorrow."

Cricket looked at Shilo and nodded. "We can do that! We'll bring you lunch tomorrow."

"That would be awesome! We'll be here." She put on her helmet and gloves.

As the kids turned to head back home, Shilo leaned close to Cricket. "Where are you going to find enough food to feed all of them?"

Cricket shrugged. "There are only eight. I'm sure we can find what we need." They couldn't do much to help the wildlife, but they could definitely help the people.

Now the kids were in a hurry to get home, but when they turned the corner, a steady stream of campers and trailers blocked their way.

"It looks like a parade—without the marching bands and horses," Shilo said. "And your dad's the marshal."

Warden McKay was directing traffic as it exited the campground. He waved the kids over.

"We're just about done here," he said. "Is everything good at home?"

Tyler described their preparations, and Warden McKay nodded. He stopped the traffic to let them cross, and they saw Shilo's neighbor, Mrs. Steeves, joining the long line of cars. She rolled down her window.

"Shilo?" Her voice quivered. "I have to go now. I've packed everything up, but"—she paused and sniffled—"but I can't find Socks. He's been missing for two days."

The girls looked at each other in dismay. Was Mrs. Steeves's cat just exploring, or had he sensed the fire like the other animals had? Was he hiding somewhere, or would he come home?

"We'll find him, Mrs. Steeves," Shilo promised.

Cricket nodded. "We'll keep looking for him. Don't worry."

Mrs. Steeves's smile wobbled as she thanked the girls. They stood back on the sidewalk to watch the long line of cars creep down the road and out of town.

Chapter Five

"We spent an hour searching for him," Cricket said as she ate a french fry. Everyone was home for an early dinner, even her dad, and they all had shared their news of the day. "Socks must be hiding somewhere."

"I hope so. I know Mrs. Steeves loves that cat," her mom said. "But can someone please tell me why half the pantry was emptied onto the table?"

Cricket froze. "Uh, well, I needed to make some lunch."

Mrs. McKay raised her eyebrows, and Cricket sighed.

"I promised the firefighters at Cameron Falls that we would bring them lunch tomorrow." She looked at her dad. "They didn't pack enough food."

Warden McKay frowned. "The crews have moved into the motel, but the support teams haven't arrived yet." He took a bite of his hamburger and chewed while he thought.

Cricket held her breath.

Finally he nodded. "That's very helpful, but where will you get the food?"

"Yes," her mom said with a bit of a frown. "*We* still need to eat too, so please don't raid our fridge."

Tyler stopped chewing for a minute. "All the stores and restaurants are closing up. They might have food they would give you."

Cricket nodded. Every so often her brother had a brilliant idea. "Giving it to the firefighters is better than throwing it away."

"Mr. Watson might have some stuff you can use." Tyler squeezed another glop of ketchup onto his plate. Mr. Watson was Will's dad, and he owned Pat's Garage, the only gas station in town. "I'm going down to help them pack up the garage tonight."

Cricket stared at her brother. They had to gather supplies tonight, or it would be too late!

She pushed her plate away. "Can I be excused? I have to call Shilo."

The girls pulled Shilo's wagon through town to gather supplies. Mr. Watson emptied an entire shelf of beef jerky into a bag and gave it to them, along with

a flat of juice boxes. The grocery store was already closed, but Mrs. Chen was packing up Pearl's Café when the girls knocked on the window.

"Do you have any food you don't need?" Cricket asked.

"Anything we could feed to the firefighters?" Shilo added.

Mrs. Chen clapped her hands. "Perfect! I didn't know what I was going to do with all this."

She reached behind the counter for a big box. "Here is everything you need for sandwiches—bread, meat, even pickles. You can give it all to them."

Cricket and Shilo smiled. "That's great! Thanks very much, Mrs. Chen. We'll make the lunches tonight," Cricket said.

As the girls started down the street with their heavy load, they heard the deep drone of an airplane. They stared up at the sky with their mouths open as two planes flew directly overhead, so low that the windows of Pearl's Café vibrated.

"Those are water bombers," Cricket said as they watched the planes disappear around Bertha Peak. "Dad said they fill up at the Waterton Dam. They must be almost done for the day." She sighed. It was too dangerous for the air teams to work in the dark, which gave the fire all night to grow.

A fire crew was working in the middle of the street, down near the marina. One of the firefighters waved as they got closer.

"Hello again, girls," Whitney said. "I see you're still working hard."

The girls nodded. They watched the crew set up an inflated yellow pool that looked deep enough for the girls to swim laps in.

"What's that?" Cricket asked. "Is it a pool for the animals to hide in?"

"No, though that has happened before. It's a relay pond. We need to pump water from the lake into the pond so trucks can refill quickly and return to work."

"But we have fire hydrants all over town," Shilo said. "Why don't you use those?"

"We are, but it's not enough for all the trucks and crews."

Cricket looked past Whitney to Pat's Garage, where another crew was setting up an identical relay pond. The noise from all the pumps and rumbling fire trucks forced people to shout to one another. Back-up alarms and whining chain saws added to the noise.

It was difficult to understand why they were working so hard. The sky was brilliant blue, and Cricket could smell only a hint of smoke. The wind still hadn't picked up. They hadn't seen any more wildlife racing through the town. Maybe everything would be fine. Maybe they'd be lucky, and the firefighters wouldn't have much work to do. But whether they had to work the next day or not, the crews would be hungry—and now there was a lot more than eight firefighters in town!

Chapter Six

When the girls arrived at Cricket's house, they found Tyler busy cleaning off the counters and table. Boxes of sandwich bags were stacked on the stove.

"I planned an assembly line with Will," he said, "and he brought all these sandwich bags and disposable gloves from the garage." Tyler frowned and shrugged. "He can't help us though. He's still loading the mopeds and bikes into their trailer."

Shilo nodded. "Yeah, I'm going to have to go soon too."

Cricket's stomach dropped into a pit of worry again. "What?"

"Not now—hopefully not tonight," Shilo said quickly. "We've got a bunch of sandwiches to make!" She opened the big box Mrs. Chen had given them and tossed a bag of bread to Tyler. "Let's get your assembly line rolling!"

Following Tyler's plan, they set up one station with sandwich meats such as turkey and roast beef, another with peanut butter, and another with extras like lettuce, pickles, mustard, cheese and jam.

The kids washed and dried their hands carefully and put on the gloves. Tyler held his hands up in front of himself.

"Nurse, where's the patient? I'm ready for surgery."

Cricket rolled her eyes, and Shilo giggled.

Shilo took a loaf of bread from the box and arranged slices on the counter.

She added roast beef, then passed the half-finished sandwiches to Cricket at the table.

"Lettuce and cheese?" Cricket asked.

"And no mustard," Tyler said.

Shilo spun around. "No mustard?" She glared at Tyler.

He threw his hands up in surrender, and a glob of peanut butter flew off his knife, landing on Cricket's shirt.

"Ah!" Cricket scraped the peanut butter off her shirt. "Gee, what's the big deal about mustard? These sandwiches are for *other* people, remember?"

Tyler apologized. "Some people feel strongly about mustard," he mumbled.

Cricket rolled her eyes. When Tyler turned back to spreading peanut butter, she added lettuce and a squirt of mustard to every roast beef sandwich.

Shilo sped up, slapping meat onto sandwiches and spinning around to pass them to Cricket like she was practicing a basketball pivot.

The competition heated up. Tyler worked faster. He swiped peanut butter left and then right with a flick of his wrist, as if he had a hockey puck on the end of

the knife. He slapped two more sand-wiches down in front of Cricket.

"Score!" Tyler shot his arms in the air and strutted in a circle just as Shilo spun around. Roast beef and bread flipped out of her hands. A slice of meat landed on his shirt, stuck for a second, then tumbled onto his bare foot.

"Ugh! That's gross!"

Shilo laughed. "Oops, sorry!"

Cricket giggled, but then she got mad. "This assembly line isn't working. You guys are working too fast!" A long line of half-finished sandwiches stretched across the table in front of her, waiting for jam or lettuce or cheese.

"I'll help," Shilo said. They worked steadily, handing the sandwiches to Tyler for bagging.

Eventually they started to run out of supplies. Tyler had three peanut butter sandwiches left when the jam ran out. He shrugged and fished pickle slices out of the jar, arranging them carefully in the peanut butter before adding the top slice of bread.

Cricket stared at him.

Shilo's mouth dropped open in surprise and disgust.

"What are you doing? Did you actually put pickles in that peanut butter sandwich?" Cricket demanded.

Tyler smiled. "Pretty good, eh? Not everybody likes sweet. Some people like salty, right?"

"That can't be good," Shilo said, shaking her head.

They had to get even more creative as supplies ran out, and Cricket wondered if anyone would actually want to eat the last few sandwiches they put together.

When they finished, the sun had set and stacks of sandwiches covered the kitchen table. It had been a long day, and everyone was ready for bed.

Chapter Seven

In her dreams Cricket couldn't escape the sandwiches. She tossed and turned until morning, dreaming about a mountain of bread that filled the kitchen. She struggled to find the mustard. She searched under loaves and lettuce, slipped on pickles and squished jam between her toes. Slices of bread tumbled toward her, like the mountain was crumbling. She was trapped. She couldn't move her legs. She heard Tyler's voice calling her from the other side of the mountain of bread.

"Cricket! Are you up?"

Up? Why would the mustard be up? She was still stuck, unable to move. She felt a hand grip her shoulder. Cricket froze.

"Cricket, wake up. It's morning. Shilo's here."

Her eyes flew open. "Did she find the mustard?"

Tyler laughed and shook his head.

Cricket struggled to sit up. She frowned. Her legs were tangled in her blankets, and she could hardly move. That was a crazy dream. Why would Tyler hide the mustard?

When she heard her mom talking to Shilo, Cricket untangled her blankets and jumped out of bed. She ran down the stairs.

"Hey," Shilo said. "I just came to say goodbye. My dad says we have to go now."

Cricket's eyes widened. "Already? We have to deliver all those sandwiches."

"You can do it, you and Tyler." Shilo bit her lip and handed Cricket a cat carrier. "This is for Socks. If you find him, you can put him in here for Mrs. Steeves."

Cricket nodded.

"There's a couple of cans of food too. He'll be hungry." Shilo gave a little hiccup. Outside a car horn beeped. Before Shilo could turn to the door, Cricket put her arms around her in a big hug.

"We'll see you really soon, Shilo," Mrs. McKay said.

Cricket stepped back. "At the pool, right?"

Shilo gave her a small smile. "Sure. At the pool." Then she turned and ran down the steps to the car.

Cricket stood on the steps in her pajamas and waved, watching Shilo's car until it disappeared around the corner. For the first time, she smelled thick smoke in the air.

Later Tyler stood in the kitchen with his arms crossed. He leaned against the counter, watching Cricket eat breakfast.

"If you eat any slower, you'll have to call that lunch," he said.

She rolled her eyes and slurped another spoonful of cereal. She would much rather crawl back into bed and hide under the covers, but they had sixty-seven sandwiches to deliver. They would have had sixty-eight, but Tyler had eaten one of the weird ones just to prove they were good. Like peanut butter and pickles could be good.

While she finished her cereal, Tyler packed all the lunches into their backpacks and the baskets on their bikes.

"Dad said we should start at the Prince of Wales Hotel, then make some stops in town," he said.

Cricket nodded glumly. Their dad had been out of the house and up in a helicopter before she'd even gotten out of bed, and their mom was at the warden's office, coordinating radio communication. The plan was very clear—make their deliveries, then get home to grab their go bags. Grandpa would pick them up in a couple of hours and take them to the farm, which was just outside Pincher Creek. They would be safe there, out of the path of the fire.

She pedaled behind Tyler, who seemed excited by everything that was happening. Two days ago evacuation had sounded like fun to Cricket—but not now. Now Shilo and Will were gone, Socks was lost, and Mom and Dad were busy trying to save the town. She put her head down to pedal hard, and a big fat tear slid down her nose.

The road to the Prince of Wales Hotel went up a short, steep hill. Cricket was grateful for the gentle breeze giving her a little push as she pedaled. They rode into the parking lot and stopped. Two big fire trucks were parked close to the hotel. Painted on the trucks' doors was the fire-department crest CFD. This crew was from Calgary, more than three hours away! As she walked closer, Cricket felt her chest vibrate with the rumble from the engines.

"Wow." Tyler watched the ladder extend from one of the trucks. Three firefighters rode it higher and higher, shooting foam from a huge hose. Big chunks of foam broke away in the wind, but most of it landed on the wooden balconies of the hotel.

A firefighter on the ground noticed the kids and left the crew to meet them.

"We have lunch," Cricket explained, opening her backpack. In no time the kids were surrounded by firefighters.

"Hey, this sandwich has peanut butter and pickles!"

"This one has tuna and chips. I love tuna and potato chips!"

Tyler looked over at her with a big grin, and Cricket rolled her eyes. Firefighters from Calgary were probably the only people on earth who liked the same weird sandwiches as Tyler.

While the crew members chose their sandwiches and got beef jerky from Tyler, Cricket watched a line of water bombers returning to fill their bellies at Waterton Dam. Movement in the grassland area near the road caught her attention. It was a huge herd of elk—there had to be hundreds of them! They walked in quick circles and stayed tightly together. Their heads were high and their necks were stiff.

Then they ran.

Before Cricket could call to Tyler, the elk were gone. They ran away from the fire and out of Waterton Lakes National Park.

Cricket walked behind the hotel. From the hill she could see the entire town. Not a single car or tourist roamed the streets. No campers or motorhomes, and no smoke from the cookshacks. The streets were dotted with fire trucks, though, and lines of yellow hose lay like a giant spiderweb over the town.

The tangle of worry in Cricket's stomach grew to fill her chest.

The only people left in the town were firefighters.

Chapter Eight

"Cricket!" Tyler was waving his arms, trying to get her attention. One of the firefighters stood beside him, talking on his radio.

"What's wrong?" Cricket asked, coughing.

"That was your dad," the firefighter said, clipping the radio back onto his shirt. "It's time to evacuate. Make your last delivery and then get home to meet your grandpa." He paused as water bombers roared past. "The wind has picked up, and the fire is moving fast. If they can't stop it, your dad thinks the fire could be at the townsite in four or five hours."

Cricket was frozen for a moment, her mouth open in a surprised O. Four or five hours? That meant the fire had jumped the ridge and was coming down the valley. The tangle of worry exploded, shooting energy into her arms and legs.

"Okay, let's go!" She zipped her backpack and jumped on her bike. Tyler threw on his backpack, and they took off down the hill into town.

They rode their bikes down the middle of the street to the marina. Tall sprinklers perched on roofs, shooting jets of water onto buildings and trees. Everything dripped.

The kids rode around a rumbling fire truck and found the crew crowded together, studying a map. Firefighter Whitney gave them a quick wave, and

the wind almost ripped the map from her hands.

"What are you two doing here?" she asked.

"We're leaving right away," Cricket said, "but we brought lunch."

Whitney peered into Cricket's basket and grinned. "Right on!" In seconds the kids were surrounded by a dozen firefighters.

As Cricket handed out sandwiches, she spotted movement near the playground. A doe and two fawns bolted from the shadows, heading toward the lake. The mother bounded across the grass, over some driftwood and onto the rocky beach. The fawns struggled to keep up. The first one scrambled over the driftwood and followed its mother into the water, and they began to swim.

The second one slid and fell. When it got to the water, its mom was already swimming.

The fawn ran back and forth, its tiny hooves splashing in the water. It bleated and cried. The doe turned around and bleated to it, then continued to swim across the lake. The fawn jumped into the water, but the wind and waves knocked it down. It struggled to swim, but its head slipped underwater.

"It can't swim!" Cricket cried. She took off at a run, jumping over the driftwood and into the lake. The water was over her knees when she reached the fawn. She reached down and scooped it up, then carried it to the beach.

Cricket searched the waves for the doe, but she was far across the lake with the other fawn.

Tyler knelt beside the fawn and put his hand on its side. The fawn was panting and starting to shiver.

"I've never seen anything like that!" Whitney handed Cricket a blanket. "Do deer normally swim like that?"

Cricket nodded as she gently rubbed the fawn. "Lots of animals swim across the lake," she said.

"It's a long way to walk around it, but less than half a mile to swim across from here," Tyler said.

Whitney's radio squawked. She listened for a minute, then stood up, looking back toward Crandell Mountain. "Ten-four, Warden McKay. Both kids are here at the marina."

Cricket and Tyler listened. Their dad spoke quickly. Wind was pushing the fire faster than expected, and the road into town was closed. The fire was coming *now*.

The kids looked at each other, eyes wide. Grandpa couldn't come to get them.

Dad was somewhere in a helicopter, and Mom was at the warden's office, just outside of town. They were cut off from help and couldn't evacuate!

Whitney turned to the kids as she reclipped her radio. "We'll keep you safe here, but you'll have to stay out of the way," she said.

Cricket's mind raced. Grandpa could pick them up if they could just get out of town. Wasn't there another way out?

She looked at the fawn, thinking, then turned toward the marina, searching for the familiar flat green roof and Canadian flag. "The boat! Could we take Dad's boat?"

Tyler nodded. "We can do that. We can evacuate by boat!"

Whitney frowned. "I told your dad I'd keep you safe."

"You can drive the boat," Tyler said. "I bet the keys are in it."

"That would be awfully lucky," Whitney said, then radioed Warden McKay again. While she talked, she eyed the cloud of smoke that loomed over the mountain. She looked at the kids and then at the boat. "Ten-four. I'll take them to the north boat launch. Over."

Tyler jumped up. "Okay, let's go!" He sprinted for the marina.

Cricket looked down at the fawn. It was stranded, just like them, separated from its family. She knew her dad wouldn't be happy, but she couldn't abandon it now.

She wrapped the fawn in the blanket and tucked its legs in tightly, so she wouldn't be kicked by the tiny hooves. Only the fawn's wet black nose poked

out of the blanket. Cricket stood up,
cradling the awkward bundle in her arms.

"We're ready."

Whitney opened her mouth, then
closed it, nodding. She turned and
followed Tyler to the marina.

Chapter Nine

Once Whitney steered the boat out of the marina, the ride got rough. Wind made the water choppy, and the boat bounced along. Ice-cold water blew up in their faces. Looking back, Cricket watched fire trucks racing through the town. Mist blew from all the sprinklers. She looked up. High on the bluff, the crew showered the Prince of Wales Hotel with water. Behind the hotel, the dark cloud of smoke hung over the mountain. It was lit by an orange glow, like a sunset, though it was the middle of the afternoon. Cricket saw a flash of flames coming down the valley.

"Watch for embers," Whitney yelled over her shoulder. She had warned them that branches and even whole trees could be blown upward by the inferno and flung far ahead of the fire. The wind was driving the fire hard and fast.

Cricket hugged the fawn and searched the shore, looking for Grandpa. She knew it was a short trip around the bluff—not more than fifteen minutes—but it seemed to take forever. Trees bent in the wind, reaching toward the lake as though trying to escape the fire that was roaring down the mountain. Then she saw Grandpa standing on the boat launch, waving his arms over his head.

Whitney slowed the boat. Grandpa waded into the water to help Tyler to shore. His eyebrows shot up when Cricket handed him the bundled blanket.

He turned and passed it to Tyler, then reached back for Cricket.

Cricket looked at Whitney. "What about you? Aren't you coming with us?"

Whitney shook her head and looked back toward the town. "I have to get back to the crew. They need me there, and you're safe now."

Cricket nodded, then surprised Whitney with a hug before she climbed over the side of the boat into Grandpa's arms. At that moment, with Grandpa's strong arms around her, she did feel safe. Suddenly she was very tired.

Cricket woke up as the truck turned onto the long driveway to Grandpa McKay's farm. Grandma and Cooper,

Grandpa's old border collie, stood outside waiting for them.

"The barn is ready for your little orphan," Grandma said as she helped Cricket climb out of the truck, holding the fawn.

Cooper sniffed the blanket, and his tail wagged slowly. He followed right behind Cricket. She unwrapped the fawn in the barn, in a cozy space Grandma had prepared with straw and a heat lamp. The fawn looked around, then curled up under the warm orange glow of the lamp. Cooper slowly crept in and lay beside the fawn. He put his chin on his paws and looked up at them.

"Good boy, Cooper." Grandma led the kids out of the barn and closed the door. "He's used to the new calves we have every spring. He'll take care of the little guy—don't worry."

The kitchen smelled of melted cheese and toast when they walked in, and suddenly Cricket was starving. Grandma's grilled cheese sandwiches were the best. Cricket reached for a second sandwich as a news update interrupted Grandpa's fishing show on TV. Pictures taken from a helicopter showed smoke hanging thick on Crandell Mountain. The bits of forest they could see above the town were completely black and burned.

Cricket and Tyler looked at each other. What about their town? What about Mom and Dad?

The news reporter on the TV was on the ground, outside the park warden office.

The camera turned—and suddenly there was Dad! Cricket's heart jumped.

DEVELOPING SITUATION
FIRE REACHES EDGE OF WATERTON
ON THE SCENE

"*The fire swept down the mountain very quickly,*" Warden McKay told the reporter. "*Usually fire moves more slowly downhill, but the wind pushed flames through the treetops. The fire came right up to the edge of town, and crews are still working hard to make sure it's out.*"

The camera moved to show more of the scorched forest. In some places the trees were completely gone, and the earth was smoking.

"There's Mom!" Tyler pointed to a spot behind the reporter, where some firefighters were talking.

The kids cheered. Their family was okay.

But what about their town?

Chapter Ten

A week later Tyler poked his head into the barn. "Dad called—it's time to go," he said.

"What?" Cricket turned around, but he was already gone. The fawn moved to grab the bottle of milk, stepping on Cricket's foot.

The fawn had learned how to drink from a bottle and had grown quite a bit in just a few days. His tiny hooves were still sharp, though, and Cricket winced as he stepped on her toes in his eagerness to finish lunch.

"You'll be back home soon, buddy," she said. She had to resist patting his soft, spotted fur. Her mom had warned her not to get attached to the fawn and not to name him. He wasn't a pet and had to be returned to the wild.

Cricket sighed. "I just hope your mom and brother are there," she whispered. The forest would be a dangerous place for the fawn on his own.

It didn't take long to pack up. Cricket and Tyler stuffed their backpacks with the extra clothes and toothbrushes their mom had brought them, and they were off. The fawn was lying in a box on the back seat, beside Cricket.

Their mother drove slower as they got close to the park gates. She had warned them that everything would look different. The firefighters couldn't clear away everything the fire had burned—they had to let nature heal the forest.

Cricket stared out the window with wide eyes. Everything was black. Tree trunks stood without branches, like black toothpicks stuck in the black ground. Guardrails lay on the side of the road beside their charred posts.

In the bison paddock, one lonely bison stood up to its knees in the wallow, surrounded by a carpet of singed black grass. A little farther on, Beaver Pond looked completely fine. Long reeds and

cattails waved in the wind, and the water sparkled. Past the pond, though, everything turned black again. The road to Red Rock Canyon was closed, blocked by barriers her dad had probably put up.

Cricket squinted and blinked. What was that covering the road?

"Whoa, snakes," Tyler said. "That is so weird."

As they drove closer to the stable, Cricket gasped. Everything was gone. The fences, the hitching posts and even the barn—all gone! The trees and bushes were black all the way up the hill. At the top was a small oasis of grass, and in the middle stood the Prince of Wales Hotel. The fire trucks and crews had left days earlier, and the hotel stood all alone, looking over the lake. Across the road Crandell Mountain was black. Not a speck of green was left. Cricket held her breath as they drove down Salamander Hill and into the town.

When the truck turned the corner, Cricket let out a little sob.

Long green grass grew on every lawn. Every cabin was standing. She could see Pat's Garage down the street and the Canadian flag flying at the post office. Their house looked just like they had left it.

Cricket blinked. Was that Socks sitting in the window?

When their mom stopped the truck, both kids threw open their doors and raced across the lawn.

"Dad!" Cricket shrieked as he threw her up in the air like he used to do when she was little. He put her down and wrapped Tyler in a big hug.

"I missed you two. It was awfully quiet around here without you," he said with a wink.

Cricket grinned. "We saw you on the news," she said.

"Lots of times," Tyler added. "You were getting pretty good at answering all those questions."

Warden McKay raised an eyebrow. "Oh, was I? So happy you thought so."

He trapped Tyler in a headlock and ruffled his hair. "Go unpack your bag, Mr. Smarty-pants."

When Cricket turned to follow her brother into the house, her dad put a hand on her shoulder. "Not you, Cricket. You and I have a job to do."

Cricket's smile vanished, and her heart sank. "But what if..."

He shook his head, and she followed him slowly to the truck.

She had known this would happen. She knew she couldn't keep the fawn. She knew her dad was very angry that she had taken it with them during the evacuation. But the fawn was all alone. How could he have survived?

Her dad drove to the marina and parked. The relay ponds and fire hoses were gone, but she saw two fire trucks way down the street. It was quiet without pumps and engines rumbling or airplanes roaring overhead.

Cricket sighed. "I'll do it, Dad."

The fawn was curled up in the box, sleeping. Cricket tried not to wake him as she slid the box off the seat and walked through the park to the shore of the lake. This was where his mom had left him—was there any chance she had come back? Was there any chance she was waiting for him to come back?

The fawn woke up as she put the box down. He jumped out and sniffed the grass. While he investigated, Cricket walked back to the truck. She quietly closed the door and watched as the fawn looked at the lake, his big ears flicking forwards and back.

"He remembers," she whispered.

The fawn swung his head side to side and bleated. He turned in a quick circle, then looked at the truck and bleated again.

Cricket gave a little sob, and her dad wrapped his arm around her shoulders.

The fawn walked to the lake and put his nose in the water. He bleated again, loudly, calling for his mom.

Cricket's dad nudged her shoulder and nodded at the bushes. A doe hesitated, then stepped out into the park. Was it her? Was it the fawn's mom? Cricket couldn't tell.

The fawn sprinted across the grass and slid to a stop. The doe froze, neck stiff and ears back. She looked ready to run. The fawn gave a little cry and lifted his nose toward her. Cricket held her breath.

The doe's ears twitched. With a sigh, she relaxed and lowered her nose to the fawn.

"That's a very lucky fawn, Cricket."
Her dad started the truck and drove slowly
down the street.

Cricket wiped her cheeks and smiled.
They were *all* very lucky.

Epilogue

In September 2017 fire really did race down the mountain into Waterton Lakes National Park, right up to the edge of town. That fire was started by lightning in an area so remote and steep that firefighters had little chance of stopping it. Crews from seventeen fire departments worked hard to protect the town and historic sites, fighting flames pushed unbelievably fast by high winds. The fire was finally put out by rain and snow.

Fire can be devastating and destructive. Within the forest, though, fire is an important and natural part of an ecosystem's life cycle. Trees like lodgepole pine *require* fire to stimulate new growth. Grasses will begin to grow just a few days after a fire, green shoots pushing through ash. The first flowers to bloom will be glacier lilies, fireweed, lupines and bear grass. Woodpeckers will arrive to feast on beetles in dead trees. Fast-growing, lush grasses will attract rodents, deer and other browsers, which will eventually be followed by predators such as cougars and wolves and then scavengers.

But will the forest regrow? Will it return to what we remember? Probably not, and certainly not within our lifetime. It will be twenty years before trees are taller than hikers and one hundred years before they are full size. Climate conditions following a fire will determine if forests will even grow at all or be replaced by grasslands. For scientists and environmentalists, fire provides an exciting opportunity to watch the ecosystem change and rebalance as nature heals itself.

Pamela McDowell's first career was in education, teaching junior and senior high school. She began writing when she left teaching and has now written more than fifty fiction and nonfiction books for children. Pamela grew up in Alberta and enjoys writing about the diverse animals and habitats of her home province. She lives in Calgary with her family. *Fire on the Mountain* is the fifth book featuring Cricket and her friends.